THE BIGGEST PUMPKIN EVER

THE BIGGEST PUMPKIN EVER

by

STEVEN KROLL

Illustrated by JENI BASSETT

SCHOLASTIC INC.

New York Toronto London Auckland Sydney
Mexico City New Delhi Hong Kong Buenos Aires

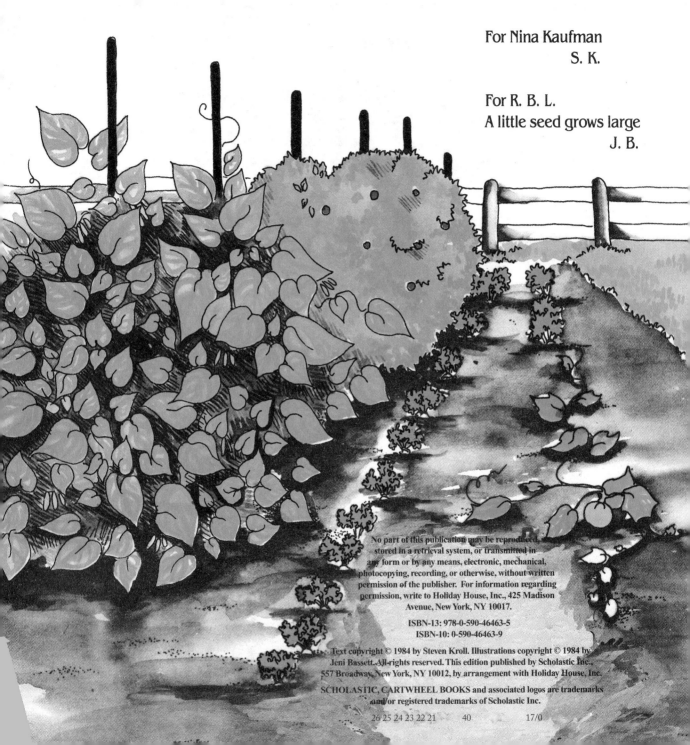

For Nina Kaufman
S. K.

For R. B. L.
A little seed grows large
J. B.

ISBN-13: 978-0-590-46463-5
ISBN-10: 0-590-46463-9

Text copyright © 1984 by Steven Kroll. Illustrations copyright © 1984 by Jeni Bassett. All rights reserved. This edition published by Scholastic Inc., 557 Broadway, New York, NY 10012, by arrangement with Holiday House, Inc.

SCHOLASTIC, CARTWHEEL BOOKS and associated logos are trademarks and/or registered trademarks of Scholastic Inc.

26 25 24 23 22 21   40   17/0

Once there were two mice who fell in love
with the same pumpkin.

Clayton the house mouse noticed it one day in the vegetable garden. It was still little and green, but Clayton thought he could make it grow really big. It might even get big enough to win the grand prize at the town pumpkin contest.

Desmond the field mouse discovered the pumpkin the same day. He thought that if he helped it grow, it could become the biggest jack-o'-lantern in the neighborhood.

That afternoon, Clayton watered the pumpkin. He also mixed up some fertilizer of manure and water. He spread the mixture around the pumpkin to make it grow larger.

That very same night, Desmond went into the garden. He watered the pumpkin, too. He also spread some manure mixed with water around it.

The next day, Clayton watered
and fertilized the pumpkin again.

The next night, Desmond did the same.

And the pumpkin began to grow.

By the end of a month, the pumpkin was so large,
Clayton couldn't believe his eyes.

"My goodness," said Clayton's mother. "And it's not even full grown."

Clayton shrugged. "All I do is water it," he said.

Clayton's mother whispered in his ear. "If you want the pumpkin to grow bigger faster," she said, "you should use sugar water."

That night, Desmond brought his brother Morris to see
the pumpkin. Morris knew everything there was to know
about growing things.

"That's some pumpkin," he said.

Desmond shrugged, "All I do is water it," he said.

Morris whispered in his ear. "You should try using sugar
water," he said.

The next day, Clayton dug a small hole beside the
pumpkin vine. In the hole he placed a bowl full of sugar
water. He cut into the vine a few inches from the pumpkin.
In the cut he put one end of a piece of candle wick. Then he
put the other end in the bowl of sugar water.

That night, on the other side of the pumpkin, Desmond
did exactly the same thing.

Within a week, the pumpkin was twice the size it had been

Within two weeks, it was absolutely enormous!

Clayton was amazed. He ran down the road and peeked
into his friend Jimmy's pumpkin patch. The pumpkin Jimmy
was growing for the contest looked much smaller.

Clayton scratched his head. "I have an amazing pumpkin,"
he said out loud, "and I think I'm going to win the contest."

That night, Desmond and his brother Morris spent a
long time looking at the pumpkin.

"How do you think it got that big?" Desmond asked.

Morris shrugged. "A little luck, a little skill."

"It's going to make some jack-o'-lantern," said Desmond.

"It sure is," said Morris.

A week later, Clayton noticed the pumpkin was bigger than the family car. During the day, everyone he knew came by to admire it.

And at night, all the field mice gathered round to do the same.

By now, summer was almost over. In a week the pumpkin would be full grown and start turning yellowish and then orange. A few weeks after that, it would be ripe and ready for the pumpkin contest.

Clayton could hardly wait. The pumpkin was growing so fast, it would soon be larger than his house. Then he had a terrible thought. If the pumpkin was so big, how would he get it to the contest? It wouldn't fit in his red wagon. It wouldn't even fit in a truck.

Clayton decided to worry about this when the time came.

That night, the weather grew colder. Thinking there might be an early frost, Clayton rushed out to the pumpkin with his blanket. One was not enough. Soon he was rushing back and forth, carrying all the blankets from the house.

As he worked, he hummed a little song, and as he hummed, he heard someone else singing. He also began to realize that someone else was covering the pumpkin with blankets.

Desmond, too, had seen the danger of an early frost. He, too, had brought blankets for the pumpkin. And as he worked, he sang a little song. And as he sang, he began to realize that someone else was working and humming.

Clayton stopped humming. He put down his pile of
blankets and peered around the corner of the pumpkin.
Desmond stopped singing. He put down his blankets
and peered around the corner of the pumpkin.

The two of them bumped heads and fell down.
"You've been feeding the pumpkin," said Clayton.
"You've been feeding the pumpkin," said Desmond.
"That's why it got so big," said Clayton.
"That's why it got so big," said Desmond.
They burst out laughing.

When everything had been explained, Clayton said, "I know I'll win the contest if I can get the pumpkin to town."

Desmond smiled. "I'll help you. Just let me carve the pumpkin into a jack-o'-lantern for Halloween when the contest is over."

"It's a deal," said Clayton.

"A deal," said Desmond.

And they shook on it.

The morning of the contest was bright and sunny. Mice were bringing their pumpkins to the town square by truck and car and wagon. Some were rolling them along the ground.

Suddenly they all stopped short. Over the fields, came the biggest pumpkin anyone had ever seen. It was being pulled by a hundred field mice on motorcycles.

When the pumpkin reached town, it was too big for any of the streets. Clayton had to explain why they couldn't bring it to the square.

The mayor understood at once. He led the crowd to the
giant pumpkin and pinned the first prize ribbon on its
side. Then everyone danced around it.

"Who would have believed this?" said Clayton as he danced.

"Who would have believed this?" said Desmond at the
same moment.

When the celebration was over, the hundred field
mice pulled the pumpkin back to the field. The day before
Halloween, they carved it into the best jack-o'-lantern ever.

And on Halloween night its wonderful, smiling face
could be seen glowing for miles around.